Tsey

Gasant

"Bones! Wouldn't it be fun to plant a dinosaur garden?"

"Did you know that some dinosaurs ate nothing but plants?"

"Things like fern, ginkgoes, pine, magnolia..."

"Giant asparagus. Broccoli. That should attract some dinosaurs."

"First we dig a hole."

"Next we drop in a few seeds."

"Then we water..."

"Yikes!"

"Where are we??"

"This looks just like the time of the dinosaurs!"

"Bones, I'll bet there are plant-eaters here!"

*"We're *all* plant-eaters!"

"Look, an egg—I wonder who it belongs to?"

"Is it yours?"   *"No!"

*"No!"   "Yours?"

"Is it yours?"   *"No!"

"Yours?"   *"No!"

*"Mama?"

"Isn't it cute? It looks like…"

*"Run!!"

"Aaaah!! A baby Tyrannosaurus!!"   *"Mama!"

"... And it's a meat-eater! Help!"

"Wow!"

"Thank you!"

"Look, Bones. Is that another egg?"

"Let's take it home."

"I wonder what kind of egg it is?"

GLOSSARY

ANCHICERATOPS (ANG-kee-sair-a-tops). *Similar horned face.* This dinosaur was 16 feet long. It had three horns on its head and a large sheet of bone called a frill, to protect its neck. This plant-eater had strong teeth and jaws for eating tough plants.

BRACHIOSAURUS (BRAK-ee-uh-sawr-us). *Arm lizard.* With a neck half its 75-foot body length and very long front legs, this dinosaur stood taller than a four-story building. Brachiosaurus probably ate the leaves from tree tops that no other dinosaurs could reach.

HETERODONTOSAURUS (het-er-uh-DON-tuh-sawr-us). *Different-toothed lizard.* Named for its unusual teeth, this dinosaur had short front teeth for cutting, broad teeth for grinding, and long canines for defending itself. Heterodontosaurus was three feet long.

LEPTOCERATOPS (lep-toe-SAIR-uh-tops). *Delicate horned face.* This plant-eater was seven feet in length and walked on all four legs. It had clawed fingers on each hand and a sharp beak-like mouth for cutting leaves and twigs. Leptoceratops had a paddle-like tail possibly used for swimming.

MAIASAURA (mah-ee-ah-SAWR-uh). *Good mother lizard.* This duck-billed dinosaur was 26 feet long and probably walked on two legs. The discovery of Maiasaura included an entire nesting site, with egg fossils, hatchlings and several adult fossils. This gentle plant-eater probably nested in groups.

PARASAUROLOPHUS (par-ah-sawr-OL-uh-fus). *Similar crested lizard.* At 33 feet long, this dinosaur had a huge six-foot crest. This crest may have been used to make unusual calls to signal others of its kind. A plant-eater, Parasaurolophus probably weighed three or four tons.

POLACANTHUS (po-luh-KANTH-us). *Many spines.* With heavy armor plating, this plant-eater had projecting spines on its shoulders for protection from predators. It was 13 feet in length.

PTERODACTYLUS (tair-uh-DAK-til-us). *Wing finger.* Not a dinosaur, but a flying reptile. Named because the leading edge of the wing is formed by one long finger. It had a small body and two-foot wings made of skin. Pterodactylus was probably a fish and insect eater.

TYRANNOSAURUS (tye-RAN-uh-sawr-us). *Tyrant lizard.* At 39 feet long and 20 feet tall, Tyrannosaurus was one of the largest meat-eating dinosaurs known. It had 60 daggerlike teeth that were three to six inches long, and very weak arms that were too short to reach the mouth. (It ripped at carcasses with little help from its hands.)

PLANTS Plant life near the end of the age of dinosaurs was not much different than it is today. Scientists can speculate on what plant life was like and what plant-eaters ate by studying the contents of dinosaur stomachs; by recording the plant fossils found near dinosaur fossils; and by understanding the kind of teeth that plant-eating dinosaurs had.

EGGS It is believed that most dinosaurs hatched from eggs. Many different types of egg fossils have been discovered. They vary in size and shape: some are round, some are potato shaped, some are shaped like a football, and all are relatively small compared to their parents! As yet, no Tyrannosaur (or Tyrannosaurus) eggs have been found, so it is hard to know exactly what they may have looked like.

For Grace, Nina and Eden.

With special thanks to Dr. Paul Sereno, Assistant
Professor, Department of Anatomy from the University of
Chicago, for fact-checking the glossary.

A LUCAS · EVANS BOOK

Copyright © 1990 by Liza Donnelly
All rights reserved. Published by Scholastic Inc.
SCHOLASTIC HARDCOVER is a registered trademark of Scholastic Inc.

No part of this publication may be reproduced in whole or in
part, or stored in a retrieval system, or transmitted in any
form or by any means, electronic, mechanical, photocopying,
recording, or otherwise, without written permission of the
publisher. For information regarding permission, write to
Scholastic Inc., 730 Broadway, New York, NY 10003

Library of Congress Cataloging in Publication Data
Donnelly, Liza.
Dinosaur garden / Liza Donnelly.
p.   cm.
Summary: When Rex plants a dinosaur garden to attract dinosaurs,
an unexpected guest comes to dinner.
ISBN 0-590-43173-0
[1. Dinosaurs — Fiction.   2. Gardens — Fiction.]   I. Title.
PZ7.D71955Dhe 1990   [E] —dc20   89-33737   CIP   AC

12 11 10 9 8 7 6 5 4 3 2   0 1 2 3 4 5/9

Printed in the U.S.A.   36

First Scholastic printing, March 1990

DINOSAUR GARDEN

by Liza Donnelly

SCHOLASTIC
HARDCOVER

SCHOLASTIC INC.
New York